I0571154

A Trick Of The Light

A Fairy Tale About Knowing
by Brendan Myers

NORTHWEST
PASSAGE
Books

Gatineau, Quebec

A Trick Of The Light
by Brendan Myers

ISBN (Print edition): 978-0-9939527-1-5

Published by
Northwest Passage Books
Gatineau, Quebec, Canada

For all enquiries, please visit
BrendanMyers.net
or
Fellwater.ca

~ Acknowledgements ~

In April and May of 2014, the Hidden Houses series of novels was the subject of a successful fundraising campaign on Kickstarter.com, a popular internet-based crowd-funding platform. More than five thousand dollars was raised from 144 supporters to pay for professional editors and designers.

I wish to thank all of my project backers for their generosity and support, not only with their money, but also with their time promoting the project. In particular, I wish to thank these outstanding benefactors and world-builders, each of whom donated $100 or more to the project: Carole Martin, Ben Rossi, David LeBer, Gary Gibson, Laurent Castellucci, David LeClerc, and Ezekiel Zong-Han Azib.

For Marie-Claude,
who asked me to write something like this.

Happy Midwinter!

A Trick Of The Light

Eleven-year-old Jillian Brighton liked to take the short cut to school in the morning. It gave her time to kick away the piles of carefully raked autumn leaves on the curbside, or climb up a sign post and turn the street names to face the wrong way.

Sometimes she would detour through an elderly neighbour's back yard to play with Laika, his husky-terrier, for a while. If the old man saw her he would yell at her and try to chase her off. She crossed his yard anyway because she could outrun him, and Laika sometimes ran with her. To Jillian, the chase was a game, and when she won she tossed her wavy brown-black hair over her shoulders like a movie star, and blew the old man a kiss.

Some days, like on this day, she took the short cut through the yard of an old empty house on a corner near the school. Some of her classmates would play there in the morning, though all their parents and teachers told them not to. That is why something fun would almost always happen there.

The empty house was the only one of its kind on the block: a former farmhouse, perhaps a hundred and fifty years old or more. A neighbourhood of plastic-siding bungalows grew up around it, one by one over time, until it was surrounded by the modern world. At its property line, the modern world ended and an older world remained.

In that older world, children could climb the parapets of half-collapsed balconies and jump down into piles of leaves, and build forts in the trees from which to throw pine cones at each other, and run around the many maples and through the dusty rooms for Capture the Flag, Red Rover, and Hide and Seek.

Each morning and evening, Jillian would go there to meet her friend Johnny-o and a score of other girls and boys from the school. They dared each other to climb the stone walls and peek into the second story windows, for the stairs had collapsed long ago, to see if anyone was hiding there. Should anyone get hurt, he shouted for a moment, and perhaps picked a fight with whomever might have caused it, only to be friends again five minutes later. The scars of scraped knees became badges of pride. To Jillian and Johnny-o, the empty old house was their castle, and the village of Fellwater was their kingdom, and they themselves were heroes.

That morning, Jillian noticed a long black car parked nearby. It faced away from the house, and its tinted windows made it impossible to see any passengers.

"Ever seen that before?" Jillian asked her friend.

"What, that car?" was Johnny-o's answer.

"That one—" Jillian replied, just as the car's engine rumbled to life, and its wheels carried it away.

"We better get to school," Johnny-o decided. "That car might have been the principal. Or the police. Or even the Prime Minister!"

*   *   *

That afternoon, when Jillian and Johnny-o passed the empty house on their way home, there was a woman sitting on a flat part of the roof. She wore a scarf that covered her hair, and a blouse, trousers, and boots in a style that Jillian had never seen outside of a storybook. Her cloak was lavishly embroidered with stars and comets and crescent moons.

Straddling a ridgepole on a tripod beside her, sat an antique bronze telescope, wide and fat and gleaming, set inside three concentric wooden rings. The woman gazed into its eyepiece with a serious expression, and looked up only to scribble something in a notebook on her lap.

"Never seen her up there before. Who is she?" asked Jillian.

"Dunno," Johnny-o replied. "Never seen her before neither. What's she doing up there?"

"What's it look like she's doing?"

"I can see what she's *doing*, you idiot, but why is she doing it?"

"It *is* kinda weird to be looking at the sky with a telescope during the *daytime*."

Johnny-o stared a little longer at the woman, and then gently nudged Jillian toward the house and said, "Jillian, go on up there and ask her."

"You ask her," Jillian replied.

"No, you do it," Johnny-o insisted. "Everybody says you're the nicer one. You ask her."

Jillian was irritated, but called to the woman anyway. "Hey, up there! Hello! What-cha doing?"

The woman gave no indication that she could hear Jillian's voice at all. Jillian called out a few more times, but no response from the woman acknowledged her.

Johnny-o nudged Jillian with his elbow. "Throw something at her."

"I'm not doing that," Jillian replied.

"You don't have to hit her with it. Just make a little noise. Get her attention." Johnny-o put a pebble into Jillian's hands and said, "See if you can hit the telescope. Then we'll run for it."

"You do it then."

"Your a better shot than me."

Jillian rolled her eyes, then took aim and sent the pebble flying. It bounced on the slate shingles close to the woman, and vanished; and as before, the woman made no sign of having seen it. Johnny-o gave Jillian another rock to throw, but it too landed just short of its intended victim and disappeared.

Johnny-o eventually pushed Jillian toward the house. "Climb up there," he told her.

"Why me?"

"Cause if you don't, I'll tell everybody you were afraid."

"I've climbed to the roof of that house a hundred times."

"You have not! Nobody's ever gone higher than the balcony. If she can do it, then— Are you scared of an old woman?"

Jillian folded her arms and turned up her nose. "I'm not scared of anything! I just don't wanna go."

Johnny-o sighed, and looked around for a while, and fiddled his finger in his ear. Then he played his final card, and whispered in her ear, "We're the Wild and Troublesome Two!"

Jillian grinned, replying, "Getting in Trouble is What We Do!"

She leapt up to the rickety old cedar that leaned over the house and climbed into its heart. She reached out from one of the stronger branches, and stepped on to the half-fallen balcony. Up she scrambled on hands and knees, over to the wall, and the hole where the balcony door used to be, where the ancient wood no longer groaned ominously beneath her weight. From there she clambered around the stones to a nearby gable, and the little ledge that was the benchmark of bravery, the highest point on the house that any Fellwater kid had ever dared to climb.

"There's no way to go any higher!" she shouted down to Johnny-o.

"How did that lady get up there?"

Jillian looked around as best she could. There was an old metal drainpipe that she could climb, if she was careful. She pulled on it experimentally, to see if it could support her. It rattled a bit, and scratched the stones with its anchors, but it held in place. Jillian decided that it was better to risk falling to the ground than to risk Johnny-o telling all his friends she was a coward. Upward she pulled herself, one slow pull at a time, until she could reach the eavestrough. Then she swung her young legs up like a monkey. She was on the top roof, grasping precariously to its ancient slate shingles, fearing the fall to the ground for the first time.

The woman with the telescope was just across the other side of the gable. At last she looked up, at first with curiosity, and then with a cheerful smile.

"Hello there, young lady."

Jillian found the woman's acknowledgement surprising, and she suddenly became unsure of what she was trying to do.

"Um, hi there," she said.

"Come sit on the platform, it's safer," the woman offered.

Jillian backed away. "I'm sorry, I should go." Then she bent her head down slightly, so that her brown-black hair would hide her face, and she could pretend she wasn't there.

The woman grinned brightly, and said, "My name is Professor Olivet Omari, and I'm a scientist. What's your name?"

"I better go," Jillian said, and turned back to the drainpipe and prepared to shimmy down to the earth again.

Instead, she gasped for a breath and gripped the ledge tighter. When she looked down, it seemed as if the house was a hundred feet off the ground. Johnny-o was too small and distant for his shouting to be heard. Birds flew beneath her, and clouds floated by, and in the distance she could see the farm fields and the trees of the conservation park outside the village. Jillian looked to Olivet for an explanation: her face and gaze had to pose her questions, for her voice had stuttered away.

"That's what I love about rooftops," Olivet acknowledged with a bright grin. "You can climb up here, and leave all the desperate absurdities of life beneath you, and then it's just you and the sky. And all the things that really matter suddenly become clear." When she saw that Jillian was still clutching the ledge fearfully, she added, "Don't worry. When you climb down again, everything will be just as it was when you climbed up."

Jillian scrambled up to a safer ledge on the roof, and looked from one landmark to another.

Olivet stretched out her hand invitingly, and said, "Come on over here. Don't be afraid. I'm looking at a new comet with this telescope here. It has three tails. Three tails! No one has ever seen the like before! Would you like to see it?"

Jillian scrambled across the roof and accepted the professor's invitation. The telescope's eyepiece showed her a sheet of early twilight colours: blue, purple, and red. Two or perhaps three feeble stars picked out the only sharp details. Between them lay a thin whitish smudge.

"Can you zoom in closer?" asked Jillian.

Olivet adjusted a setting on the eyepiece, and Jillian looked again. The smudge was more clearly a comet now, with a bulging head, and a long misty tail. Olivet adjusted another setting on the telescope, and two more bright tails sprang into view: one orange, one yellow, both of them brighter than the white tail between them.

"Whoa, that's— that's really—" Jillian stumbled her words. Then she noticed that while she was busy looking into the telescope, the sky had become the same shade of purple and red as she saw in the eyepiece, and that stars were emerging even as she watched. Olivet looked up to them, smiling to herself, relaxed and comfortable with the sight. Jillian's eyes scanned the scenery, still impossibly far below, and she thirsted for something familiar and ordinary to look upon.

"I have to go home," she stuttered. She scrambled down the roof slope again, and howled as the drainpipe swung like a pendulum when she grasped it, and jumped to the balcony and then inside the ancient house through the balcony door. On safer footing, though every floorboard creaked noisily beneath her, Jillian ran for the front door and then for the nearest great old maple tree that she could hide behind.

Johnny-o trotted over and said, "What's wrong with you, Jillian? Didn't you hear me shouting at you?"

"No," Jillian whispered, with a quick and shaking breath. Then she peeked around the tree at the house, although she moved carefully, as if she didn't want the house to see her looking.

Then Johnny-o noticed Jillian's condition. "What happened up there?" he asked.

"Nothing," Jillian answered.

"Nothing? Then why are you so scared?"

"I'm not," Jillian asserted, although she was still grasping the tree, and her knuckles had turned white with the effort.

"You are! You're a scaredy-cat! Jilly the scaredy-cat!"

"Don't call me that!"

"Then go on up there again."

Jillian felt a slight tremor of weakness fall through her body. Johnny-o's threat stung more than the fear, so she stood up, let go of the tree, and said, "I already did go up there. You go this time. It's your turn."

Both of them looked up to the roof of the house again, but this time they saw nothing more than three crows, perched on the spot where Olivet's telescope once stood.

"The weird lady is gone now anyway," said Johnny-o, as he tossed a pebble into one of the empty windows of the house.

"Might as well go home then," said Jillian.

"Race you to the lawn bowling place!" shouted Johnny-o, and then both of them were off, fleet footed as rabbits, and over the shallow dips and gentle rises of the road they knew so well, from the school and the empty house to the bowling green. From there Johnny-o continued on toward his house, while Jillian turned on to a side road that led home. She ventured one quick glance over her shoulder at the house, but its peak was now concealed behind the maple trees, and Jillian decided that there was probably nothing more to see.

*   *   *

That night, Jillian protested that she should be allowed to stay up past her bedtime, because the thunderstorm would keep her awake anyway. But her mother would not have it. So Jillian found herself lying in bed, wide awake, counting the seconds between each lightning flash and the thunderclap that followed it. According to her father, counting that way could tell her how far away the lightning was, and whether the storm was getting closer. And it might help her get to sleep.

Jillian's window overlooked a typical postwar brick house across the street. Tonight she saw it only in silhouette against a backdrop of low storm clouds, lit from the orange streetlights below. Beyond it, a few blocks away, she could sometimes see one gable of the old abandoned house, but only in the winter, when the trees had lost their leaves. Jillian crept to the window, her blanket over her shoulders, to see if the rough winds of September had torn off enough leaves to open a line of sight to the house. She wanted to reassure herself that there was nothing strange or wrong about it, and nobody sitting on its roof.

A flash from a distant lightning stroke showed her Something was out there: a silhouette with a telescope, perched on the ridge pole of the house across the street, and looking back at her. Jillian gasped and jerked herself away from the window. She caught her breath and dared herself to look again. She peeked slowly around the frame, ready to snap away to safety if *something* was still out there. This time, nothing unusual appeared; all was as it should be. So she went back to her bed, and sat quietly for a while, thinking about what the woman might have been doing on the house across the road. When that became boring, she took a pen light from the bedside table, and shined its beam on each of the homemade model planets that hung from a mobile on her ceiling. There was the sun, a fuzzy yellow tennis ball, in the centre; a pebble from the driveway for Mercury; a ball of orange yarn for Venus; and blue and green yarn for Earth. Then she looked out the window one more time.

Another burst of lightning flashed into the bedroom, and with it came the brief image of the woman with the telescope. This time she seemed to be stepping off the roof of the house across the road, and floating across space toward her. Jillian gasped, and burrowed under the blankets, her arms and legs curled up, her back to the window. She started counting again, and waiting for the thunder. One, two, three, four- The further away the lightning, she told herself, the safer she was. Seven, eight, nine, ten- and she relaxed somewhat, and let her face come out from under the blankets. Thirteen, fourteen, fifteen, sixteen- and now, there came the thunder, feeble and quiet and harmless, sixteen miles away. Carefully, Jillian crept back to the window and looked out. All was dark: in the last lightning strike, the street had lost power. She could hear her parents downstairs complain about the interruption of their movie, and fumble about in search of candles.

Then someone knocked on the front door.

*   *   *

Jillian jumped out of the bed, ran to the top of the stairs, and warned her parents: "Don't answer it!"

Jillian's father, who had his hand on the doorknob, turned and said, "What's the matter, Jillian?"

Jillian's words came out in a rush of confused stuttering. "It's the weird woman who was sitting on top of the old house and she had a telescope in the daytime and she couldn't see us or hear us even when we threw stuff at her and then I climbed up to the roof of the house and I'm sorry I know I'm not supposed to do that but I did and everything up there was wrong it was like the house was suddenly a hundred feet tall so if you open it that might happen to our house so don't open it please don't please please don't!"

Jillian's mother stepped on the bottom stair and said, "Don't be silly, Jillian. It's probably just a neighbour who wants to borrow a flashlight."

"It's not a neighbour it's the woman from the old house and if you open the door she'll come in and everything will change so please don't please don't!"

"Change in what way, exactly?" asked her father.

"I don't know," Jillian replied.

"Then that's enough, Jillian. Go on back to bed."

The knocker at the door knocked again, and a lightning flash revealed the silhouette of the woman, standing on the very threshold of the house.

"Don't open it!" Jillian pleaded.

"To bed, Jillian!" her mother commanded. Her father opened the door.

Jillian grasped the railing on the stairs and squeezed.

No person stood on the threshold when the door was fully opened. Instead, Jillian and her parents found a large antique wooden trunk. Rain dribbled in little streams between the round wooden ribs on its lid. A yellow envelope, sealed with a red wax seal, sat on top. The three looked at each other in puzzlement. "Well, bring it in and shut the door," her mother said. "You're letting the heat out."

The crate was easily as large as Jillian herself if she curled up in a ball. It was fairly heavy, so her father asked for help to wrestle it inside the house. Her mother told her to fetch some towels so it wouldn't scratch the floor.

When they had it in the living room, Jillian's mother sent her to bed again, but her father invited her back down again. He was examining the envelope with the seal, and seemed troubled by it.

"Jillian, do you know who might have left this here?" he asked.

"The woman from the empty house, that I told you about."

"So who is she, and how does she know your name?"

"I didn't tell her my name! Honest!"

"Then why does this letter have your name on it?"

In the soft glow of the candle light, Jillian saw that her name was spelled out on the envelope, in fine calligraphy.

"Jillian, is there anything you're not telling us?"

"No, honest! I climbed up to the top, and she told me her name, and I know I'm not supposed to talk to strangers so I climbed back down again."

"What was her name?"

Jillian thought for a moment, and then said, "She said she was a scientist."

Father examined the envelope again and said, "I've never seen this kind of seal before. Wonder what it is, and what it means."

Jillian reached for the envelope and said, "Can I see?"

Father handed her the envelope. The seal showed something like a tulip flower surrounded by calligraphy, but she could not read the writing.

Mother said, "I think we should not open it until we know where it came from."

"Why shouldn't we open it?" said Jillian's father. "After all, it's addressed to Jillian."

Mother acquiesced. "Open the letter first then. If it's from some kind of stalker, we keep the box closed, and we call the police."

Jillian cracked the seal and opened the envelope. Inside she found a page that was not quite paper, but not quite cloth. In elegant calligraphy, the letter said:

> *Open your windows, and look far and near,*
> *Who knows what wonderful things will appear?*
> *Climb to your roof-top, and look near and far,*
> *Who knows how looking will change who you are?*

As Jillian read the last line aloud, the locks on the trunk unlatched themselves, and the lid opened itself. Jillian's mother stepped back, and put a protective hand on Jillian's shoulders. Her father stared in awe until hot wax from the candle he was holding fell on his bare hand.

"Whoa!" Jillian exclaimed.

"Don't touch it!" her mother warned.

Jillian was excited now, and so she ran ahead, and reached into the chest to retrieve her treasure. There she found an old copper telescope, shimmering in the candlelight. The three large setting-wheels which supported it on the tripod had several embedded rings, and were marked with numbers, letters, pictograms, and other mysterious symbols. On the telescope cylinder itself there were various knobs and gears that held additional lenses, or which changed the focal length, or which did something else that Jillian didn't understand. Although she could not tell for sure, she thought it was the same telescope she had seen Olivet using, on the roof of the old house.

"What on Earth is that?" exclaimed her mother.

"Careful with that, my girl! It looks like an antique. It must be worth a fortune," said Father.

Jillian was a little bit worried now, too. She looked out the nearest window, in case the world had changed again, as it had on the roof of the old house. With the power failure, it was too dark to see anything.

"Now we really have to find out who this came from," said Mother.

Jillian set the telescope down in the centre of the living room, and started to assemble it, with Father's help. Only then did it occur to her that with the tripod attached, it was bigger than the interior of the chest in which it was delivered. She looked at the chest, and saw that the interior was lined with ordinary wood, and it might have been only the candlelight that made it seem deeper on the inside than its height should allow. She looked to the letter again, to see if there was any clue in it about who it came from. The poem had disappeared, and in its place was a more straightforward message:

> *This Etherial Cosmographic Telescope*
> *is the property of*
> *Miss Jillian Brighton,*
> *A gift from her friend Dr. Olivet Omari,*
> *Professor of Esoteric Geography,*
> *Secret University of Anatolia.*

"Etherial cosmographic telescope, eh? Looks like an ordinary telescope to me, although an expensive one, I'm sure," said Father.

"We can't keep it," Mother decided. "We should put it somewhere safe until we can return it to whomever sent it."

"But it belongs to me now! Look!" said Jillian, and she showed her mother the letter.

Mother frowned as she read it. "I don't know. I think you're too young to play with something like this."

"What do you mean, I'm too young?"

"Jillian, my dear, you might be as tall as me now, but you are still a little girl. You should be baking cookies for your grandmother. Not reading science books and building model spaceships."

"What's wrong with me reading science books and building spaceships?"

"Nothing, of course. There'll be a time when you're ready for grown-up things. But that time doesn't have to be today. It's okay to be a little girl, a little while longer."

"How much longer!" Jillian demanded.

Mother smiled wistfully and said, "Just a little longer."

"You know," said Father, "A mysterious stranger who delivers a fancy telescope like this, in the middle of a thunderstorm, in the middle of the night— that's kind of like a fairy tale."

"You're not helping," Mother retorted.

Father sighed and said, "Well, tomorrow we should write to that university and ask them what's going on. It's hard to believe that a stranger would just give you a free telescope like this."

"Well, can I use it a few times before we send it back?"

"Not tonight, Jillian. It's raining!"

"Not anymore. Look!"

Jillian's parents opened the living room curtains and found that the rain had indeed stopped. The sky was still full of clouds, but some spaces for the stars were opening between them, and a half-moon illuminated them with its silvery light.

Mother said, "Nevertheless, it's late. You have school in the morning."

Father helped her disassemble the tripod and stow it back in its trunk. As the two of them carried it to a store room in the basement, Jillian said, "The storm is gone away now. And the power's still out. It's darker than it's ever been. So it's like— the *perfect* night to use a telescope!"

Her father smiled and shook his head. "There will be other dark nights. And maybe for your birthday we'll get you a telescope that's really your own."

Jillian protested that there would never be a night as dark and perfect as this night, but she protested all the way to bed.

*   *   *

With her alarm clock dead, and the whole world dark, time seemed folded into an eternal 'now': she might have lain awake in bed for ten minutes or a hundred years.

When she heard her father snoring, she crept down to the basement to retrieve the telescope. With every turned corner and every creaking door, she stopped to listen, in case her movements woke her parents up. The only sounds she heard were the normal creaking of windows and walls as the cool air of nighttime descended upon them. As quietly as she could, she carried her prize to the back yard, along with a backpack full of sketch paper, pencils, and cookies stolen from the cupboard. She assembled everything in the corner of the yard furthest distant from her parent's bedroom windows. Checking one last time for any sign of adult supervision, and finding none, she grinned.

She pointed the telescope's rangefinder straight up in the air. She didn't have any idea what to look at first. But she wanted to look at *something*. Everything about the completely quiet night and the deep dark sky above her— its glittering canopy of smiling stars, more all at once than she had ever seen before— seemed to invite her curiosity, to encourage it, to welcome it, to demand it.

Jillian's first few observations, however, disappointed her. She certainly found things that were interesting: with the help of a simple star map in a school science textbook she found the Crab Nebula, the Horsehead Nebula, the Andromeda Galaxy. She didn't see anything that she might not have seen with an ordinary telescope. The Etherial Cosmographic Telescope was undoubtedly powerful, but it wasn't living up to its name, whatever that name meant. Still, she felt disappointed.

Then she looked more closely at the three large wheels that held the telescope in place. Each were inset with several moveable rings, some marked with numbers, some marked with letters in what she assumed were Latin, Greek, and Arabic, and others marked with symbols of objects, plants, animals, and geometric shapes. As she turned these rings while gazing through the rangefinder, things changed.

Sheets of colour rose and fell; nebulae changed shape before her eyes; asteroids and comets flew by. These discoveries were still very hit-and-miss: sometimes she would turn a wheel all the way around and nothing different would appear. Sometimes the telescope would point itself slightly off where she put it, as she turned the axis wheels. It was as if the telescope adjusted itself to find the nearest celestial object that best fit the settings she had defined. She still had to do most of the work herself, but now she felt she knew how the telescope worked.

Jillian looked at the moon. It was easy to find and almost certain to change in the telescope's different settings and ranges. It was low on the horizon now, and only half-full.

As she aimed and focused the lenses, she noticed that a spread of small orange lights dotted the dark half of the lunar landscape. The lights were mostly laid out in long straight lines, but at intervals they were gathered in clusters. The largest clusters of lights appeared where the lines converged. She turned a crank on the telescope which rotated a new primary lens in place, so she could zoom in and study the lights more closely.

"Just like roads and towns and cities," she whispered to herself.

That night, she stayed up as late as she thought was safe, knowing she had watchful parents. She drew maps of the civilization on the moon, and wondered what the people up there looked like.

At school the next day, she fell asleep in class.

*   *   *

When school was over for the day, Jillian ran straight to the abandoned house. She was still tired, but she was excited about her discovery, and she wanted to share it with the professor on the roof of the empty old house.

When she came within sight of the house, she saw the same long black car parked beside it which she had seen the previous day. This time it was accompanied by two pickup trucks. She heard the knocking and banging of people inside the house, and saw the glints and twinkles of flashlights in the windows. A man with a brown suit, white shirt, red tie, and a walking stick, stood by the black car, apparently supervising the people in the house. Jillian thought he cast a shadow that looked like a bull ready to charge.

When he saw her slow down and stop running, he greeted her with an open hand. Jillian thought his hand was too grasping, and his smile was too full of teeth.

"Excuse me, little lady," he said to her. "Do you live around here?"

Jillian felt annoyed by the man's use of the words 'little lady', and she stepped away.

Johnny-o came running down the street at that moment, and he called out, "Hey, Jillian! Is the woman with the telescope back again?"

Then he saw the man speaking to her, and stopped running. At the same time, two other men emerged from the house, carrying an extension ladder. They told the first man that they found nothing on the second floor, and they were going to check the roof next.

"What's happening?" Johnny-o asked Jillian.

The man looked to Johnny-o and said, "What was that you were saying about a woman with a telescope?"

Jillian folded her arms and said, "Who wants to know?"

"Nicholas Brogger, private investigator. From your local chapter of The Guardians International. Ever heard of us?"

"Oh yeah," said Johnny-o. "Your meeting house is on the street where I live."

"Wonderful!" said Nicholas. "Would you like to join the youth wing? I could sign you up right now."

Jillian rolled her eyes, then said, "You had questions for us?"

"Yes," said Nicholas. He cleared his throat and asked, "About this woman with the telescope who you mentioned. We're looking for her. You see, we think she stole that telescope from us, and we're here to recover it."

Johnny-o answered first. "We saw her on the roof of this house yesterday. And then—"

"—And then we went home," Jillian finished for him.

Johnny-o gave her a puzzled look. "No we didn't. You climbed up on the roof and—"

"—And nothing happened," Jillian finished for him again. She grabbed his arm and turned to walk away.

"Jillian, what the hell?" Johnny-o complained.

Nicholas stepped in front of them both, and drew a photograph from inside his jacket, saying, "Is this the woman you saw here yesterday?"

Johnny-o said, "Maybe, but I can't be sure. She was too far away."

"How about you?" Nicholas asked Jillian.

"No," she told him, and she started walking away, and pulling Johnny-o along with her.

Nicholas smiled. "So, I'll take that as a yes. Any idea when she will be back?"

"No!" Jillian shouted over her shoulder, without breaking stride.

Nicholas watched her go for a while. He put the picture back in his pocket, and said to one of his assistants, "Have someone at the office find out who that little lady is."

*   *   *

The Troublesome Two arrived at Jilllian's house, and entered through the garage. Jillian paused before continuing through to the kitchen. Her parent's voices carried through the half-opened door, and they were arguing about something. They were not shouting, but they were clearly unhappy. She heard her mother say, "I searched the internet for twenty minutes, at least. And I found nothing about this 'Secret University of Anatolia'. I'm beginning to think there's no such place."

"But that telescope came from *somewhere*." Her father's voice.

Jillian crept closer to the door, and crouched down. She heard the sound of a chair moving as someone got up or sat down at the table.

"But we already agreed we were going to get her some new clothes for her birthday this year."

We can still do that, but she's going to want her own telescope now, and she won't be happy unless she gets one."

"That telescope is not even the *real* problem," said Jillian's mother. "The real problem is— did you know that some of her friends are using the F word all the time now? And some of them have taken up smoking? And *some* of them—"

"I get the picture," her father interrupted. "Were we any different when we were kids?"

As Jillian's parents continued their discussion, Johnny-o took Jillian's hand and crept out of the garage. When they reached the driveway, Johnny-o said, "Best to come back later, when they're done shouting at each other like that."

"They're not shouting," Jillian said.

"Not yet," said Johnny-o. "But anyway. That telescope. Is it the same one we saw at the house yesterday?"

Jillian took her friend's arm and led him around to the side of the garage, where she was sure no one passing by would see or hear her. "Can you keep a secret? A really big secret?" she asked.

Johnny-o grinned. "Of course I can."

"It *is* the same telescope. And it's mine now," she explained.

"How did you get it?"

"The lady on the roof gave it to me. Look!" Jillian opened her backpack and took out the letter from the professor which accompanied the telescope, and showed it to Johnny-o.

"I took it out last night," Jillian continued excitedly. "And I looked at the moon for a while, and I saw this!" She showed Johnny-o the diagrams she had drawn of the civilization on the moon.

"Craziness!" whistled Johnny-o. He looked over the letter with wide-open eyes. Then he said, "Wait a minute. There's nobody living on the moon. Everyone knows that. There were twelve people who walked on the moon, once. But that's all."

"I'm telling you what I saw," Jillian countered.

Johnny-o looked at the letter from Olivet and said, "And this university. Didn't we just hear your mum say it doesn't exist?"

"Mum only said she couldn't find it. That doesn't mean it doesn't exist," Jillian insisted. "Why don't you believe me?"

"Because. People see stuff that's not real all the time. Like puddles of water on the highway, on hot days. Or things you see in your dreams. Or anything on reality-TV. Maybe the telescope is designed to play tricks on you. Like a kaleidoscope. It just shows things through filters and weird colours."

Jillian folded her arms and grimaced. "Well I say that my telescope shows me the truth," she declared.

Johnny-o was still doubtful. "But if you're the only one who saw it," he said, "then how does anyone *else* know you're not making it up? Come on, Jilly! Pics or it didn't happen!"

Now Jillian was almost to the point of shouting. "I'm not making it up!" she insisted. "Right now there's an actual weird-science telescope in a treasure chest in my basement. It has to have come from somewhere. And I know what I saw when I pointed it at the moon."

"Look," said Johnny-o, as he pulled a book out of his backpack. "Remember that story we read in class today? The one called *The Gargantacore*? I'm reading the next one in the series. It's called 'The Secret People'. And here, it talks about your telescope. There's even a character in the book who looks like the woman we saw on the roof of the house yesterday."

Jillian grabbed the book and looked. She found a diagram and a description of the Etherial Cosmographic Telescope, just as Johnny-o said. It was kept in the same kind of wooden trunk, and was operated with the same three axis-wheels. Jillian put the book down, wandered back to the sidewalk, and leaned on a tree.

Johnny-o followed her and said, "So, I'm sorry, but even if I believed you, nobody else would. It's just a story in a kid's book. That's all."

Jillian looked to the distance for a while, lost in thought. When she heard Johnny-o packing his backpack and preparing to go home, she said, "But you saw the scientist on the roof. You saw her, just like I did."

"Yeah, I did," Johnny-o confirmed.

"Well, then," Jillian smiled. "Think you can sneak out of your house at midnight tonight?"

"Sure, easily. Why?"

"Meet me at the old house. We'll see if she's there again."

"What if she's not there?"

"She'll be there."

*   *   *

Jillian opened the window of the second-floor bathroom, and crept on to the roof of the garage. A pine tree in the corner of the back yard, and a rickety wooden fence, served as a ladder by which to reach the ground. She scampered across the yard and ducked through a narrow path in the cedar hedgerow that separated her back yard from the neighbour's yard. She glanced back at her house, to be sure none of the windows had lit up: that would be a sign that her parents noticed her escape. Seeing no such warning, she dashed between two neighbour's houses, and she was on her way to her midnight appointment.

Jillian once boasted to Johnny-o that she could reach the old house blindfolded; she knew the lay of the village so well. Tonight she was in no danger of getting lost, but she moved carefully nonetheless. A young girl in a small town had little to fear by day; but Fellwater was a different place after dark.

Many streets in the older part of the village had only one or two working streetlights. Often, the tall autumn trees crowded them, giving them haloes of maple red or elm yellow. These islands of warmth were surrounded by long reaches of midnight blue, full of the clicking of raccoon claws on the pavement, and the fluttering of bats in the air. Near to her destination, a group of high school boys gallivanted across her path, on their way from the downtown core to the school playground. She hid beneath a rosebush as they passed, but not simply to avoid being seen. Her new knowledge, and her purpose, opened for her a different world then theirs. She didn't want intruders to dispel it.

Once the boys were far enough away, Jillian resumed her midnight mission. Arriving at the house, she hid herself beside a pile of leaves, safe from the eyes of night time dog-walkers, and car headlights, and boys. Her hiding place gave her a clear view of the moon. Contemplating it, she noticed the strangeness of its everyday face.

Johnny-o arrived after a few minutes. He dashed from shadow to shadow like a hunted animal, instead of creeping carefully, as Jillian had done. Jillian forgot her wariness of witnesses, and a glint of mischief returned to her eyes. When Johnny-o was close but not too close, she tossed a pebble at a tree, to divert his attention away. He followed the sound of the pebble-fall, and then Jillian whispered his name, with drawn-out vowels, like a cartoon ghost: "Johhhhnnaaathaaannn! Johnathan Waaaalllllleeeerrrrr—"

"Who's there!" a slightly panicked Johnny-o whispered back.

"I'm waaaatchiiiing youuuuu—"

"Is that you, Jillian?"

Johnny-o looked around the yard for the source of her voice. When he was close enough, Jillian reached out and grabbed his ankle. Johnny-o jumped, and reflexively kicked back. Leaves scattered in the air. Jillian stood, and threw the leaves back in his face.

"You should have seen yourself, you were completely freaked out!" she laughed.

"No I wasn't! And don't ever do that again!"

Jillian laughed again, and then remembered that both of them were not supposed to be there, especially at night. She took him around the corner of the house, and they sat together on the edge of the porch.

"Is the weird lady up there again?" asked Johnny-o.

"I didn't see her when I got here," Jillian answered.

"You gotta climb up there again."

"Why me every time?"

"Because I told my dad about the lady we saw here yesterday. And he told me not to play here again. I'll get in trouble."

"I thought you liked getting in trouble! 'We're the Wild and Troublesome Two - Getting in trouble is what we do!' Remember?"

"Yeah, but, you know," Johnny-o lamented, and then looked away.

"Fine, if you're not gonna go, then I will," Jillian announced.

As she crept around the house, in search of an angle where she could see the roof but remain mostly hidden from the road, she saw a blue-tinted soap bubble float down from above. It landed on a pine tree branch, and let out a little chime as it burst, like the tinkle of a tiny bell. Jillian looked up to see where it came from, and found another bubble, green-tinted, floating toward her. She touched it with her finger, and it burst with another bell chime.

"Johnny-o, come here! You gotta see this!"

As Johnny-o came running, Jillian saw Olivet Omari on the roof again. This time the strange scientist was holding up a large soap-bubble ring on the end of a rod. A light breeze was blowing her bubbles for her. Beside her on a small tripod stood a device that resembled an accordion-box camera, with lots of extra dials, gages, and clockwork bells, and two reels of film winding through it, apparently recording the lazy drifting of the bubbles.

"What's she doing?" asked Johnny-o. "And these bubbles— they're moving against the wind! That should be impossible. Right?"

"Well, it must be possible, because it's happening. I wonder how. I wonder why."

Johnny-o suddenly grinned and said, "Bet you I can catch more of them than you can!"

The two troublemakers ran about the yard like much younger children at a birthday party in summer, and they pricked every bubble that fell their way. Johnny-o counted his bubbles as he burst them. Jillian discovered that the size and colour of the bubbles corresponded to the musical sounds they made when they burst. So she selected her bubbles deliberately, trying to make a song. Together they laughed with the nonsense of it all.

When the wind changed and the bubbles floated elsewhere, Johnny-o looked up to the roof of the house again, and said to Jillian, "Okay, go on up there and ask her what she's doing."

"Why should I? It's your turn!"

"Because. You said she gave the telescope to you, not to me."

"I think *you're* the one who's scared, now."

"I'm not scared, I just - She doesn't know me. But she knows you."

"Fine," Jillian conceded, and she stamped her feet stubbornly all the way to to the climbing-tree.

When she arrived on the roof, Olivet was happy to see her, and waved her to sit closer again. "Jillian, my friend! Come and blow bubbles with me!" she invited.

Jillian was going to ask about the telescope, and the university that didn't exist, and so on, but she was curious about the bubbles now. So she accepted Olivet's bubble ring and said, "If you're a scientist, then these bubbles are part of an experiment, right?"

"That's right," Olivet grinned.

"So what's the experiment about?"

"Well, a few miles from here, in the conservation park outside the village, there's a very special place, you might call it a place of power, and it's called Fellwater Grove. The laws of nature work a little bit differently there. So I'm testing to see if these bubbles behave differently when they get close to it."

"They really *are* acting strange!"

"I know! Isn't it interesting!" Olivet grinned with excitement. Then she pointed to the device sitting next to her and said, "I'm recording their movements with this Electro-Phlogiston Camera. Later on, I will compare the results from today to the results I found in other places. Maybe someday people will use my data to discover new places of power, just like the one outside of town."

Jillian thought about her explanation for a moment. "Is that what you were doing with the telescope yesterday?"

"Yes, exactly! My theory is that if the stars look different here, maybe they'll look different in the same way near another place of power."

"Tell me about this Fellwater Grove. What's it like? Can we go there?"

"Oh, I'm sorry to tell you they've had a change of management recently, and they're not really accepting visitors anymore," Olivet lamented.

Jillian held her bubble-ring high, and watched the breeze make bubbles with it. This time they floated toward the conservation park and its hidden grove. They soon became distant flecks of colour on the blue-black horizon, and then they joined with the stars. Then Jillian remembered her questions.

"Will people ever live on the moon?"

"I don't know. Maybe. What makes you ask?"

"I was looking at the moon through the telescope last night. And I saw lights on the surface, that looked like highways and cities. You know, a bit like looking down on earth from outer space. I was wondering how the telescope works. Is it a kind of time machine? Or do you think people live there right now, but only the telescope can see them?"

Olivet put down her bubble ring and gave Jillian her full attention. "That's very interesting. I've never seen signs of life on the moon, and I'm fairly sure no one else has either."

"But I saw them! I know I saw them!"

"I believe you, Jillian," Olivet reassured her. "Just because I haven't seen something, that doesn't mean it's not there. I think you might have made an unique discovery. Did you write down what all the scope settings were?"

"Yes, I did," Jillian answered proudly, and she handed Olivet a scrap of paper, torn from a notebook, where she wrote it all down.

"Good. If it's all right with you, then, I'll share this information with a few colleagues of mine, so that they can confirm your finding. If you're the first person to see what you've seen, then you will get to name it."

Jillian looked up to the moon and imagined names she might give to the settlements she had seen there. Jillian's Town. New Fellwater. Brighton Highway. Mount Johnny-o.

Her gaze returned to the earth below. She watched Johnny-o pacing around the yard. She said, "Today there was a man here, looking for you. He said the telescope had been stolen. Is that true?"

Olivet nodded, and said, "I'll tell you something about your telescope: it's been stolen and recovered many times over the years. So you should always keep it safe. Many of the people looking for it don't want to use it for science. In fact they want to prevent people from using it at all. So don't talk about it to anyone, unless it's someone you really trust."

"I can keep a secret!" Jillian promised. "But why did you give it to me? And who stole it? And who does it really belong to?"

"It belongs to *you* now, Jillian," Olivet smiled. "And it's yours because you climbed up here to find out what it was. In my world, that kind of curiosity deserves a reward."

Jillian looked up to the moon, and then said. "But— but if it's mine now, then who did it belong to before me?"

Olivet was about to answer, when she and Jillian heard the sound of a car arriving that at the house. Olivet looked down at it, and saw the driver roll down the window and start talking to Johnny-o. She frowned. "Is that the man you saw today?" she asked.

"Well, that's his car," Jillian confirmed. "So, did *he* steal it? Or did someone steal it from him?"

"The answer to that is rather complicated–" Olivet started to say. But her attention was fully on the car below. She said, "I think you should get down there, and make sure your friend is not alone with him." Then Olivet walked to the edge of the platform, and casually stepped off the roof and fell out of sight.

Jillian gasped, and scrambled to the edge of the platform and looked down. Olivet was standing on a levitating Persian carpet, and floating down to the ground, perfectly safely.

"Hey, a flying carpet!" Jillian called to her. "Hey! Wait for me!"

Olivet didn't seem to hear; she and her carpet vanished into a shadow behind the house.

Jillian sat back. Her mind reviewed everything Olivet said, and didn't say, about her telescope.

By that time, Nicholas had emerged from his car, and was searching the yard with a flashlight. He heard Jillian shouting for Olivet's help, and he shined his flashlight up to the roof, where it caught Jillian's face.

"So, she's up there with you, is she?" Nicholas shouted.

Jillian shouted back, "No, she's isn't!" It was the truth, after all.

"Did she just leave? Or are you lying to me again?"

"Why should I tell you anything!"

"Tell you what. I'll give you five whole dollars if you come down here and show me where she is."

Johnny-o perked up and said, "Five bucks! For each of us?"

Nicholas clapped his hands and said, "Only if you find her quickly!"

"I'm on it!" said Johnny-o, and he ran behind the house, to look for Olivet.

Jillian climbed down an overhang above a balcony, and said, "She's not up here."

Nicholas said, "Did you see where she went?"

Jillian only smiled and shook her head.

"Five bucks not enough for you? How about ten?" Nicholas offered.

Jillian sat down on the overhang and shifted around until she was comfortable. "This telescope you say she stole. What exactly does it do?"

"Aha!" Nicholas exclaimed. "So, you've seen it, after all. You must know how very *unusual* it is. Perhaps you know where the professor has it hidden."

Jillian shook her head and said, "Who does it really belong to?"

"Twenty dollars," Nicholas replied. "But that's my final offer. That's certainly more money than you can make in a night of babysitting."

"I'm a dog walker, not a babysitter."

"Still. Twenty dollars says you know something you're not telling me."

Johnny-o returned to the scene and said, "Twenty dollars! For both of us, maybe? Jilly, you might as well tell him what you told me."

Nicholas turned to Johnny-o, with a smile on his face. He took a twenty dollar note from his wallet and held it out for Johnny-o to see. Johnny-o reached for it, but Nicholas jerked his hand away, and said, "Tell me what she told you, and it's yours."

Jillian jumped to the ground and ran to Johnny-o's side. "Johnny, don't!" she implored him.

Nicholas grinned at Jillian and said, "You *do* know where the professor is."

"No, I don't," Jillian told him.

"In fact you probably know where she stashed our stolen property, don't you?"

"No," Jillian insisted.

"You know what's interesting about eleven year old girls? It's the age when they learn how to tell lies and get away with it. But they have not yet learned to control their giveaways. You know: a little glance to the side, a little twitch of the fingers, a little note of desperation in the voice. Someone who knows how to look for those little signs can practically read someone's mind. Well, enough to know when someone's telling a lie. You say you don't know where the professor is. You say you don't know where she hid our stolen goods. But I look at your little face, as cute as a button and as open as a book, and I know that the professor gave the telescope to *you*, to hide it from us. Didn't she?"

While Nicholas was speaking, Jillian's fingers slowly closed into a fist. When he accused her of possessing the telescope, she burst out angrily. "It's mine! The professor gave it to me! And I'll never tell you where it is!"

Nicholas grinned. "You see. I was right. Now, what's your name, little girl?"

Jillian folded her arms and said nothing.

Nicholas smiled and said, "Well, I'm sure I can find out easily enough. See you at school tomorrow."

Then he winked at her, and walked back to his car.

Jillian watched him go, her jaw open, and her hands trembling.

Johnny-o said, "Hey, what about the twenty bucks you promised!"

Jillian glared angrily at Johnny-o.

Nicholas, without turning around, answered, "You both lied to me. So I'm keeping it."

When Nicholas had driven away, Jillian shoved Johnny-o down into a pile of leaves.

"Hey, what gives!" Johnny-o complained.

"That's for trying to sell my telescope. For twenty bucks!"

Johnny-o clambered back to his feet and said, "We could have split the money!"

Jillian shoved him into the leaves again.

"Hey, stop that!" he protested.

Jillian stomped away. She went looking around the house for Olivet, and she shouted her name a few times. The professor had apparently departed. Looking up to the roof, Jillian saw that the camera and other equipment was now gone as well. When she came back around the house to where Johnny-o waited for her, she plopped herself on the ground next to him, facing her back to him.

Johnny-o said, "It isn't real anyway. That telescope of yours. It's only a thing from a book, remember?"

"I *know* what I saw, and so do you," Jillian grumbled in return.

"Okay, so I saw— I saw that woman on the roof again. And some guy who was looking for her, because of a stolen telescope. But it can't be the same one from the book. Why is this thing so important to you, anyway?"

Jillian turned around to face him and said, "Because— because— it's like this. When I was using it yesterday, I saw things in the sky that— that maybe nobody had ever seen before. It was like being let in on a secret."

"What secret?"

"I don't know yet. I think it has to do with how big the universe is, and how small we are. So small that it can feel like our lives don't matter. But it's okay. It's terrifying and it's lonely, but it's also beautiful and amazing and full of surprises."

Johnny-o thought about her words for a moment.

"Let's go back to your place, so you can show me. If the people on the moon are real then I want to see for myself."

"Not tonight. That man who'se looking for it will just follow me home, and try to take it away."

Johnny-o stood and brushed the leaves and dirt from his jacket. "You got me to come here in the middle of the night for nothing. If my dad finds out I was here, he'll be so mad he'll lock me in the basement every night for a week."

Jillian's jaw dropped. "Your dad locks you in the basement?" she said.

Johnny-o didn't stay to talk about it. "Why should you care. It'll be your fault if he does. I'm going home," he growled at her, and marched away.

Jillian watched him go for a while. Then she looked around the yard, to see if Olivet might have been watching. But she saw nothing.

*   *   *

Jillian avoided the house on her way to school the following day. Instead, she took the route that her parents and teachers preferred for her. Not that she was seeking their approval: she simply didn't want to run into Johnny-o.

The route took her along the busier streets of the village. It passed by a corner where a group of teens waited for a bus to take them to Thistletown District High School, six kilometres away. She crossed the road to avoid them: some of the boys she had seen the night before were there. While she knew it was unlikely that they would recognize her, she wasn't in the mood to deal with them. The girls at the bus stop were putting on their lipstick and eye liner. One of them was experimenting with the height of her skirt, while her friends pretended to discourage her. She noticed Jillian's fascinated stare. She smiled on one side of her mouth, careful that her friends didn't see it. Then she returned her attention to her outfit.

Jillian looked down at her own clothes: unmatched fuzzy socks, bright red tights, an autumn dress, a hooded jumper, a denim jacket. Everything she wore came from a thrift store.

She fell asleep in class again that morning. She woke with the first recess bell, and the sound of children getting up to play outside. Groggily she looked up and found her teacher, Mr. Windermere, standing over her.

"That's two days in a row now, that you've fallen asleep in class. Everything all right?"

"No it's not. I've had my telescope only two days and someone is already trying to take it away from me and my best friend doesn't believe me when I told him about it and yet he even tried to sell it to the man at the house who said it was stolen but now Johnny-o might have spent the night in his basement and it's probably my fault and and and–"

"Hold on there, Jillian. The only thing I understood there was that you went to that empty old house again. Your parents and all your teachers have told you not to."

Jillian stopped herself, and rubbed her eyes to try and shake off some of her tiredness. "Sorry, Mr. Windermere. I've just been up late, with homework, and stuff."

Mr. Windermere decided to let it pass. "I'm told that Johnny-o fell asleep in his class, as well," he said conversationally.

Jillian jumped to her feet and asked, "Where is he?"

"He's just there, in the hall, waiting for you."

Jillian ran out of the classroom. Johnny-o was holding a cardboard cylinder, painted to look bronze, and with a wider plastic cylinder on one end, representing a sun shade, and a smaller one on the other, representing an eyepiece. Various knobs and levers made of popsicle sticks had been glued on it. The main cylinder also bore the hand-written label: 'Jillian Brighton's Magic Telescope'.

"What– what's this for?" Jillian asked him.

"It's my apology. For last night," Johnny-o explained, and he put his creation in her hands. Jillian looked it over more closely, and played with the fake knobs and levers, some made from old wristwatches, one made from the dial of a cooking thermometer. She looked into its eyepiece end, and found that the lens of a kaleidoscope had been inserted into the bronze-painted tube.

"He didn't make you sleep in the basement, did he?" Jillian asked him.

"No, I got home fine. No one knew I was away," he said. Then he asked, "So, are we still the Wild and Troublesome Two?"

Jillian replied with the other half of their private motto: "Getting in Trouble is What We Do!"

Johnny-o laughed with relief.

Mr. Windermere cleared his throat to get their attention, and then said, "Now get your coats on and go play outside."

Jillian paused. "Have you ever heard of an Etherial Cosmographic Telescope?"

"I've heard of the one described in the book that we're going to read in class next week," he replied. "What makes you ask?"

"What about Esoteric Geography, or the Secret University of Anatolia?"

"I don't know much about those things either, if they exist at all. But it's easy enough to look them up. Want to spend your recess on the internet?"

"Yes, please!"

Johnny-o said, "Me too!"

The Troublesome Two searched the internet for the words 'Ethereal Cosmographic Telescope'. They were soon disappointed: all they found were some pictures of old models of the solar system from the days when people thought the earth was the centre of the universe. They found maps of various constellations, and drawings of their mythological characters. At last they found a dozen diagrams of a flat earth resting on the back of four elephants, and the elephants were standing on the back of a turtle. The more often they saw that picture scroll down the screen, the more they laughed at it.

Johnny-o said, "It's turtles all the way down!"

The search for "esoteric geography" was similarly unhelpful. When they searched for the university, they learned about a region in Turkey called Anatolia, which had volcanic formations called fairy chimneys, and secret underground cities, and other fascinating features. They found nothing about a university by that name.

"Maybe the university doesn't exist," Johnny-o concluded.

"It has to!" Jillian insisted.

"Well, the people on the moon don't exist either. So, it kinda makes sense, doesn't it?"

Jillian glared at him. Then she got an idea, and she typed 'Ethereal Cosmographic Telescope' together with 'The Secret People', and the name of the university. Most results were much the same as before, but near the bottom of the list they saw a picture of the book, and a drawing of a telescope that looked very much like the one that arrived at Jillian's home several nights ago. She clicked on the link, and read the text which appeared there:

An Ethereal Cosmographic Telescope is a scientific instrument described in the novels of Lügner Ehrlichmann, the noted nineteenth-century children's writer. In his stories, the telescope is delivered to the home of a young girl or boy who shows special curiosity about astronomy.

Johnny-o sat back from the computer. "That could be you!"

Jillian smiled, and said, "Let's see if it says anything about what it is, and how to use it."

The telescope is said to reveal correspondences between astronomical alignments, and earthly events in faraway places, or the past, or the future. Characters in the novels often disagree about the meaning of what they see, as well as about how to use the telescope properly.

"Well, that's not helpful."

"Correspondences? What are those?"

"Let's keep reading, Johnny."

Those who had the most success with the telescope used it together with a special star map called an Etherial Astrognomic Atlas, which allows the characters to set the telescope's various metrics correctly.

"So it looks like I need that special atlas," Jillian whispered to herself.

The door to the computer lab opened and Mr. Windermere stepped in. He was already in conversation with someone in the hall.

"—computers are in pretty good shape. An upgrade isn't urgent, but we wouldn't turn it down."

The person in the hall said, "The Guardians International Organization is prepared to endow your school with a very generous sum for new infrastructure. We believe in the importance of a modern education."

At the mention of the word 'Guardians', Jillian's ears perked, and her eyes fixed on the door.

Nicholas Brogger entered the room.

Johnny-o stared at Nicholas, almost frozen in his seat. Jillian looked to her teacher and shook her head, to tell him not to let Nicholas in the room.

"Children," said Nicholas. He offered a handshake to Jillian and said, "My name is Nicholas Brogger. What's your name?"

Jillian kept her hands at her sides, and said, "My parents told me not to talk to strangers."

"And they were right to tell you that," Mr. Windermere agreed. "But you can both relax. Mr. Brogger is from the Guardians. He's here to offer the school some money for new computers."

Nicholas picked up the model telescope that Johnny-o made, and smiled. "What have we here? A model of a— oh, not just any telescope, but a magic telescope. Belonging to a Miss Jillian Brighton, I see. Is that you, my dear?"

Jillian looked to her teacher, then to Johnny-o, and then to the floor. "Yes, that's— that's me," she said.

Johnny-o said, "But she didn't make it. I did."

"Did you? You must be quite the wizard. What makes it magical? "

"It's an ethereal cosmographic telescope, sir."

"An ethereal cosmographic telescope! How interesting! Where might I find a real one like it?"

Mr. Windermere intervened to say, "It's something from one of the books we're reading. I'm sorry to interrupt this, but we have only five minutes before classes resume."

Nicholas handed the telescope to Johnny-o and said, "This is an excellent likeness of the one in the book. Good job, young man."

As Nicholas and Mr. Windermere left the classroom, Jillian moved to the window, to watch her other classmates playing in the yard outside.

Johnny-o said, "I guess it's my fault that he knows who you are, now."

Jillian examined Johnny-o's model telescope, which she didn't remember picking up and taking to the window.

"It doesn't look much like *my* telescope," she said.

"I tried to make it look like the one in the book," Johnny-o explained. "I can fix it for you. What needs to be changed? Is it too long, or too short? Should I take some of these buttons and switches off?"

Jillian wasn't listening. She turned her gaze back to the window, where she saw Mr. Windermere giving Nicholas a guided tour of the school yard. Quietly, she said to herself, "I wonder why he didn't know that."

*   *   *

Jillian told her teachers she was going home for lunch, so that they would let her leave the school grounds during the noon hour break. Instead of going home, she ran to the empty house, in the hope of finding Olivet Omari again. She found the professor on the roof, talking to a robin that perched on an umbrella handle. She was listening to the bird's heartbeat and breathing with a tiny stethoscope, and measuring its wingspan and length and height with a tailor's tape, and even peering down its throat with an otoscope, all with the bird's apparent cooperation. When she finished, she gave her patient a treat and sent it on its way, and then another bird hopped up to take its place. As Jillian got close enough, she saw a line of robins standing along the ridgepole, each waiting for its turn to be examined. But when they saw Jillian, they all flew away. Olivet looked to see what had frightened them off, and when she saw Jillian she smiled brightly.

"Jillian!" Olivet greeted her. "Aren't you missing school right now?"

Jillian didn't smile back. "Where did you go last night," she demanded.

"Oh, I apologize, truly," Olivet replied. "I'll tell you another little secret. Just like you aren't supposed to be here, I'm not supposed to be here either. Isn't that exciting!"

Jillian crept closer and sat down, and asked, "Why not?"

"I'm supposed to be somewhere else," Olivet grinned. "And if certain people knew I was here, instead of there— well, for one thing, I'd lose my research funding."

Jillian said, "Last night you left Johnny-o and me by ourselves, to deal with that Nicholas guy."

"I was watching. I would not have let him harm you."

"But we didn't know that!"

Olivet nodded, and said, "I know. But if you knew I was nearby, he would know too."

Jillian wasn't fully satisfied, but she remembered that Nicholas said he knew how to tell when someone was lying. She decided to turn to other questions.

"Who are the Secret People? Are you one of them?"

"Yes, I am," the professor replied.

"So, you're not just characters in a story?"

"Everyone on Earth is a character in a story," Olivet explained. "That's why we're always telling stories. That's how we bring each other to life."

Jillian didn't seem to understand, so Olivet shifted herself closer and said, "As for we Secret People, well, we're like a very large family. With thousands of members all over the world. And some very special ancestors. You might have read about some of them: the genies of Arabia, the muses of Greece, the phantom queens of Ireland."

Jillian wanted answers to other questions. "About that detective. Nicholas. Is he one of the Secret People too?"

"No," said the professor. "But he works for one of us. Well, he works for a different branch of the family."

"He knows my name now. I guess it's only a matter of time before he finds out where I live. And comes to take my telescope away."

Olivet leaned back on her chair and thought for a moment. She said, "I can make sure Nicholas doesn't sneak into your house in the middle of the night, to steal it back. But that by itself won't be enough. We'll have to find a way to strengthen your claim to be the true owner."

"Is there anything I can do?"

"Well, to start, you should learn everything you can about the Guardians organization. Find out what kind of people they are, and what kind of work they do. Also, learn everything you can about your telescope, in case you are asked to prove that you know how to use it."

"I read that there's a special atlas that I need—?"

Olivet grinned and said, "That's right, you do need the atlas! Good of you to remind me. So, tonight, keep watch for another mysterious package that might arrive at your house. Not that I would know anything about that, of course."

Jillian smiled.

*   *   *

That evening, as Jillian washed the dishes after her family dinner, someone knocked on the front door again. Jillian ran to answer it.

"If it's another package from the same person who sent you the telescope, then we're sending it back," Mother called after her.

This time they found a smaller package, wrapped in brown paper, and tied with coarse brown string. An envelope attached to it read:

> *To Miss Jillian Brighton, of Fellwater, Ontario, Canada.*
> *The Department of Esoteric Geography,*
> *of the Secret University of Anatolia,*
> *Presents you with*
> *THE MEDAL OF MERIT FOR CURIOUS GIRLS.*
> *And with it, this gift,*
> *in honour of your first scientific discovery:*
> *The World of the Moon-People.*

Inside the envelope, Jillian found a small bronze medallion on a ribbon, featuring the official crest of the university, and inscribed around its edge with the words "Medal of Merit for Curious Girls."

"Wow, this is awesome!" she exclaimed. She hung the medallion around her neck with pride.

"This is getting out of hand," she heard her mother say.

Jillian grabbed the package and ran with it up to her bedroom, closed and locked the door behind her, and jumped on the bed to open her gift. Inside, she found a large leather-bound book, with a metal clasp holding it closed. At first she could not open it. Then she looked more closely at a seal in middle of the clasp. It looked about the same size as the medallion, and seemed to have a slot that the medallion could fit into. So she took the medallion off its ribbon and clipped it into place on the seal. Instantly it spun around with a flourish of clockwork clicks and knocks. The clasp unfastened itself, and the book opened to the front page. There, in a flowery script, above a woodcut illustration of a telescope, Jillian read the title:

The 1871
ETHERIAL ASTROGNOMIC ATLAS
of Lügner Ehrlichmann
Professor of Almost Everything,
Secret University of Anatolia.

Jillian whistled delightedly. The atlas then opened itself to the next page, which unfolded again into a long spread, almost as wide as the span of Jillian's arms. Upon it was drawn an intricate map of the night sky of the northern and southern hemispheres, with the stars in larger or smaller dots according to their brightness, the longitudes and latitudes drawn in thin lines, and the mythic images of the constellations drawn behind them in cheerful rainbow colours. Names for everything were written in a delicate calligraphy. Even the planets and their orbital paths were depicted on the map, which she thought strange, since she knew the planets were always moving. As she looked closer, she found that the numbers on the meridian lines changed every few seconds. In fact the whole map was moving. Everything slowly rotated around the pole stars.

Jillian had only moments to enjoy the atlas in private. Her parents banged on the bedroom door, and demanded that she unlock it. Mother threatened to have Father knock it down with a hammer. So Jillian quickly closed the atlas and hid it under her bed blankets. Then she unlocked the door.

"What was in that package," Mother barked.

"Just this book," she replied, and she held up her copy of The Secret People.

Father took the book and examined it. He turned to his wife and said, "I remember this book! We read it when we were kids in school." He opened the book at random and read:

The world is always wider, more beautiful, and more strange, than any one person can discover alone. So, let us climb hills,

*and sail seas, and explore! Let's look for flowers that sing like
spring crickets. Let's look for villages up in the clouds. Beyond
the next hill-crest, there may still be places where dwells
something truly, completely, amazing.*

"I always loved that part," Father concluded.

Mother let some of the sternness out of her face. "I suppose
it's harmless, then," she conceded.

"Go downstairs and finish the dishes," Father said. "Then
you can read your book all night if you want to."

As her parents left her room, she heard her mother say, "I still
don't like it. When I was her age I didn't know anything about
science, or smoking, or boys. She's growing up too fast."

"She's fine," her father replied. "When I look back on my
life, it seems as if I grew up by accident. But at the end of the
day, that's the best way to grow up. Isn't it?"

*   *   *

Jillian agreed to go to bed early that night, so that she could
read her new atlas under her bed covers with her pen light. The
introductory pages explained the origin of the telescope:

*Lügner Ehrlichmann, the brilliant Swiss mathematician-
philosopher who invented the Etherial Cosmographic Telescope,
died tragically in a shipwreck before he finished the manual for
the instrument's proper use. This Atlas was compiled by his
students, from notes discovered in his workshop, and it includes
their own discoveries.*

"But what does it *do?*", Jillian heard herself ask aloud, and
she flipped ahead a few more pages. She found her answer on
the last paragraph of the introduction:

*It is clear that the telescope reveals a sky that looks very
much unlike that which appears in ordinary instruments.
Whether it draws back the curtains of the world, or confounds us
with new illusions, or merely reveals how things could be
different, no one quite knows. The inventor himself used it to
search for worlds with no poverty, no hunger, no hate, and no
fear. He wanted to learn from such worlds, and then teach us
how to make our world better. And for this reason, the very*

existence of his Telescope is intolerable to those who benefit from injustice, and call it human nature.

Jillian emerged from under her blankets and looked out her window. Moonlight illuminated her. She thought about the civilization she had seen on the moon, and she wondered if there was another little girl in a house up there, with a telescope of her own, looking down upon the earth.

Curiosity soon compelled her to open the atlas again. Each page of the book described something new and strange in the sky, and gave the coordinates to find it. The first thing she found was a gaseous nebula, generously dusted with stars. Looking closer, she saw that all the stars in that nebula had planets, and the footnotes said that some of the planets were thought to be inhabited.

"Villages in the clouds," she whispered, quoting the passage from the book her father had read. "Planets in a nebula!"

She looked on. There were stars that whirled around black holes as fast as spinning tops. There were clouds of giant ice crystals that reflected the light in hundreds, and millions, of rainbow-scattered colours. Everywhere, there were planets. Not all were of rock and gas and ice, like the familiar planets of Earth and its companions. Some were shaped like cubes, some like flat coins, and some were hollow and resembled wicker balls. She found a planet that sprouted trees as tall as the planet itself was wide. She even found planets with eyes the size of continents, that looked out to space for another living planet to talk to. Jillian sometimes had to close the atlas and try to decide whether she really believed what she was reading there. But she never held it closed for long.

Her alarm clock eventually interrupted her. She had set it to ten minutes before midnight. That gave her ten minutes to check and see that her parents were asleep, then set up the telescope in the back yard, and meet Johnny-o there, if he got her text message from earlier that evening, and managed to escape.

Johnny-o was already waiting for her.

"You made it!" she grinned.

Johnny-o shrugged. "Dad went to the bar again tonight, so it was easy.

"My parents are asleep upstairs, so we have to be quiet," Jillian warned him.

Johnny-o examined the telescope's trunk, and said, "Is that it?"

"An official and genuine Ethereal Cosmographic Telescope," Jillian told him proudly, and she opened the trunk to show him.

Johnny-o whistled with amazement. "I didn't think it would be this big! It's as tall as me!"

"Here, I'll show you how to set it up."

With occasional help from Johnny-o, Jillian assembled the tripod, fitted the axis-wheels in place, hefted the cylinder into them, and attached the lenses and counter-balances.

"Craziness!" Johnny-o swooned, when he saw it all together. He remembered how skeptical he had been earlier that day, and decided to play it cool. "But it's just an ordinary telescope. I mean, it's old and fancy and stuff, but it's just a telescope, right?"

"Wrong-o, Johnny-o!" Jillian corrected him with a laugh. "You can see things in here that nobody's ever seen before."

"Show me the moon, then, with all the people on it."

Jillian looked down. "Actually, I've only found it once, and I've never found it again. I don't know why. I've found lots of other cool stuff, but I've never been able to find the Moon-People twice."

"That's 'cause you just made it up, didn't you?"

"I didn't make it up! But this time, tonight, I'll find it again for sure. Because I have the instruction manual now! Check it out!"

She produced the Atlas, and opened it to show the diagrams of all the strange and impossible things that the inventor and his students had found. Johnny-o pretended to be unimpressed, but a few excited sounds escaped his lips anyway.

"Look here," she said. "The book says that the alignment of symbols on these wheels affects how things appear. If you put in the right combination of symbols, the telescope will filter out some things, and make other things light up. It's like like changing the channel on a TV."

"Neat," Johnny-o smiled.

"Okay," said Jillian, "So, let me see if I can find the Moon People again. It looks like you have to start by setting all the angle-wheels at zero, and then you point the whole thing directly north— there's a compass on the tripod to show you where that is—" Then she aimed the telescope at the moon, and fixed the axis-wheels as they had been on the night of her discovery, in accord with her notes. The first view to appear showed nothing unusual at all: it was exactly the same as always. With her next attempts, she discovered a moon which was tinted slightly yellow, and was surrounded by rings of ice which glittered like diamonds. It was beautiful, but Jillian was unhappy, and she stomped her feet and growled at it.

"Still haven't found your Moon People?" asked Johnny-o, as he studied the atlas again. "It says here that even the time of day affects what you would see, and therefore the same patch of sky might look different from one day to the next, even if all the settings are exactly the same as before."

Jillian sighed and plopped herself on the ground, and pulled up a few blades of grass just to shred them.

"Now I'll never find it again."

Johnny-o didn't hear her. He was completely absorbed in the atlas. "It's because the rotation of the earth– It's like the earth itself is one of the axis-wheels! The earth is part of the mechanism! Brilliant! Crazy-brilliant!"

Jillian walked away to lean on the garden fence, fold her arms, and pout. She looked up at the moon again and complained aloud to herself, "I know I saw those city lights up there. But if I never find them again, then maybe I *did* just imagine them. Maybe nobody is out there, and there's no planets with people on them anywhere in the universe except for here on Earth. Something about that seems– I don't know. Wrong somehow. And sad."

"We still saw some pretty amazing things. Those rings around the moon?"

"It wasn't *my* moon," Jillian lamented.

Johnny-o reached over to take her hand, but she batted it away. So he lay down on the grass, flat on his back, and looked up. He said, "You know, if you lie on the ground, and put your hands around your eyes so you can't see what's around you, and then you look up at the sky, you can pretend you're actually looking down, not up."

Jillian lay on her back next to him. Johnny-o peeked at her under his hands, in the hope that she would not see him looking at her. She was looking up; and when she noticed that he was looking at her, he twitched his head to the sky again.

Jillian slowly turned to him and said, "Johnny, would it be okay if I lay my head on your tummy?"

Johnny-o took a breath before answering, "Yes, it would be okay."

Jillian shifted her shoulders and lay her head on Johnny-o's belly. Johnny-o risked putting his hand on her shoulder. This time, she did not push it away. They lay like that together for a while, looking at the stars but no longer thinking about them.

*   *   *

That was the moment when the back door opened and Jillian's mother rushed out.

"Straight to bed, young lady!" she barked.

"Mom!"

Mother pointed a judgmental finger at Johnny-o and hollered, "Jonathan Waller, what are you doing here? Actually, I know what you're doing here."

"We weren't doing anything!" he complained.

"You better go home, right now, if you know what's good for you."

Johnny-o jumped on his feet and ran.

"And I'll be telling your father everything!" Mother shouted after him.

Jillian put herself in front of her mother and said, "But really, Mom! We weren't doing anything. We were just looking at the moon with the telescope!"

"Not tonight, Jillian! And not without me and your father supervising!"

Jillian's father emerged from the house next, and began packing up the telescope. "Well, now we know why you've been falling asleep at school," he said to Jillian.

"Johnny-o had nothing to do with it!" Jillian insisted.

"Even if that's true," said Father, "you can't go sneaking out in the middle of the night."

Mother added, "Now I'm putting this thing away where you won't find it."

"Mummy, no!" Jillian screamed.

But her parents were too tired and too cross to be swayed by what Jillian thought was the self-evident truth.

*   *   *

Jillian stayed in bed as long as possible, and attended the breakfast table at the last minute. She spoke to no one, and made eye contact with no one. She sipped her cereal and plotted revenge.

Mother was on the phone with someone, and Father sat at the kitchen table, reading a book. He wished Jillian a good day, but she ignored him. She wolfed down her breakfast and then gathered her things for school: coat, shoes, books, pencil case, backpack. Then she noticed one of her books was missing. When her father saw her scurrying around the house in search of it, he leaned back on his chair, and placed on the table the book he had been reading.

"I need that for my homework," said Jillian, when she saw it.

"The Secret People, by Lügner Ehrlichmann," said Father, as he handed it back to her. "I haven't read it since I was your age, so I thought I would flip through it again."

Jillian snatched the book back, and marched for the door.

"Have a good day at school!" he said.

Jillian paused with her hand on the doorknob, and said, "Aren't you mad at me for last night?"

Father said, "For showing your new telescope to your best friend? No. For *using* the telescope, and reading science books, no. For going outside in the middle of the night without telling us, yes. If you want to do that again, you can do it on a Saturday, when your mother and I know where you are, and you don't have school the next day."

Jillian did not expect that answer. "She doesn't want me to have the telescope at all," she said.

"I'm sure that when she's off the phone, you will get an earful of it."

"But it's mine!" Jillian growled. "You saw the letter. It had my name on it. I even met the woman who gave it to me. She says I can keep it. So why can't I? I should be allowed to have a telescope if I want one!"

Father was about to answer but Mother finished her phone call and invaded their conversation. "I just had a very informative discussion with the real owner of the telescope," she said.

"From Professor Omari?"

"Who is that?" asked Father.

"She's the woman we met at the old house, remember I told you about her?"

"The person I spoke to was a man," Mother informed her. "A lawyer, in fact. He said that the telescope was stolen from one of his clients. An organization called Guardians International," Mother sternly declared. "He is coming by the house tonight to collect it."

Jillian stamped her feet on the floor. "No, Mom, it's my telescope now! The Professor gave it to me! She said so in the letter and everything!"

"This woman you saw at that house– it seems that she has stolen quite a few rare and valuable things like that telescope over the years, and the police are looking for her. If you ever see her again, I want you to come straight back here and tell me right away."

"No! I won't do it! It's my telescope and I want to keep it!"

"Jillian, I'm not arguing about this. My decision is final. The telescope will be gone by this time tomorrow."

Jillian turned to her father and said, "Well, what do *you* say?"

Father inhaled to speak, but Mother interrupted him again. "Your father and I have already agreed. The telescope goes back where it belongs."

"If you give away my telescope, I'll– I'll run away from home!" Jillian shrieked at her.

"Where would you go?" Mother retorted.

Jillian didn't know how to answer Mother's question. So Mother sighed and said, "Time for school. Get going."

Jillian didn't want to stay and argue with her mother anymore anyway. She grabbed her backpack and left, and slammed the door behind her.

*   *   *

She ran to the abandoned house, shouting for Professor Omari before she was half way there. The professor's usual perch on the roof was empty. Some of the usual crowd of local children appeared, and Jillian chased them away, in case their presence was preventing the professor from appearing. When they were gone, Jillian shouted for a few more times, and then plunked herself into a pile of leaves and leaned on a tree, to wait.

She opened her backpack and took out Johnny's model telescope, and looked through it to Olivet's rooftop platform. It made the blue and white of the sky merge with the golds and reds and browns of the trees, forming a nebulous cloud of diamonds. Then she dropped it to the ground beside her, and frowned at it, as if blaming it for Olivet's absence, and for everything else that was upsetting her at that moment. She opened her backpack again and found her copy of The Secret People, and flipped through it for a while, not really reading it. Then she dropped it beside the model telescope. She mused for a moment on the way they resembled the atlas and the telescope hidden in her home. She picked them up again, and she recalled how she had used the novel to hide the atlas, and what Nicholas had said about the model.

A smile returned to her face. She jumped to her feet again and started shouting for Johnny-o. She jogged down the street in the direction of his house, hoping to meet him on the way. She found him at the turn of the first corner.

"Hey, Johnny-o! So I have good news and bad news. The bad news is that guy from the Guardians knows where I live now and he's coming to take the telescope tonight but the good news is that I have a plan now and I think I know how to keep the real telescope hidden a little longer but I need your help and we'll have to skip school to do it but–– Johnny-o, why aren't you looking at me?"

Johnny-o kept his eyes on the sidewalk before him. Jillian touched his arm and said, "I need your help, Johnny-o. It's important. We're the Wild and Troublesome Two! Getting in trouble is-"

"Sorry Jillian," said Johnny-o.

"What's the matter?" Jillian asked.

Johnny-o didn't answer right away. His gaze swept across the street, from the parked cars on one side to the corner of the abandoned house on the other: anywhere but directly upon Jillian. When he finally spoke, he said, "My dad is gonna pick me up after school."

Jillian moved to stand in the way of where he was looking, and said, "I figured out a way to keep my telescope safe. It's a bit risky, it will only work for a little while, but maybe just long enough to– Johnny, look at me. I need your help."

Johnny-o looked at Jillian. His mouth opened and closed as he tried to speak, but couldn't work out what to say. He tried to look away again, and Jillian stepped into his field of view again. He closed his eyes. "You can't call me Johnny-o anymore, either. My name is Jonathan, you have to call me that from now on."

"What's wrong with Johnny-o?"

"It's a little kid's name."

Jillian shook her head. She turned around in a full circle, and looked at him again, and then pursed her lips and nodded.

"Your dad found out about what happened last night, didn't he?"

Johnny-o confirmed this with a nod. "He's coming to pick me up after school today, to take me straight home. And he told the teachers to tell him if we're seen together."

"So is this it? The end of the Troublesome Two?"

"I don't know," he moaned, and began walking away.

"We'll still see each other in class," Jillian added hopefully.

Johnny-o turned to her again and said, "I better go– but I wanna say– I wish that I– I wish that we– never mind. Doesn't matter. I better go."

Johnny-o did not move.

Jillian grabbed the collar of his jacket, pulled him close, and planted a quick kiss on his cheek, and pushed him away again.

Johnny-o stood stupefied for a moment, and then ran away as fast as he could.

As he ran, Jillian shouted after him. "If I can't call you Johnny-o, then you can't call me Jilly!"

*   *   *

Jillian returned to the empty house, and stood before the front door for a while, gazing at the roof, and the sky above. Then she climbed inside through one of the open windows. She scavenged the rooms for treasures, and found a stove pipe, some burnt-out fuses and light bulbs, a few handles and fixtures from broken kitchen cupboards. Despite Olivet's absence and Johnny-o's retreat, she smiled. She had a plan.

She took her treasures home. She waited at the corner of her street, to watch for her parents depart for their jobs. Then she trespassed into her own house: up the fence, then to the pine tree, then across the roof of the garage and finally in through the second-floor bathroom window. Once inside, she unlocked her father's workshop behind the garage, and she laid her treasures on the table.

*   *   *

At dinner that evening, Jillian did her best to avoid answering her parent's questions about why she wasn't at school that morning. When she finished, she ran to her room, to study the atlas again.

The hours of the evening sped by too fast. A heavy pounding on the front door told her that the work was about to begin. She crept downstairs and saw that her parents were watching the television in a kind of trance. The screen alternated between a flashy and hypnotic design, and various affirmations written in tall and colourful letters: YOU ARE RIGHT ABOUT EVERYTHING, and YOU ARE BEAUTIFUL, and YOU ARE SAFE AND PROTECTED, and YOU DESERVE TO WIN.

"Mom? Dad? There's someone at the door," said Jillian. Her parents remained fascinated by the television. Jillian passed her hands before their eyes, but they did not respond. Then she smiled: she realized this was the professor's way to make sure her parents didn't interfere with what she needed to do.

The man at the door was Nicholas Brogger. He still seemed to stand ten feet tall, and his shadow now resembled a hooded mediaeval executioner holding a huge axe. Jillian reflexively stepped back.

"Hello Jillian. Nice to see you again," he smiled, and Jillian thought he had pointed teeth and a forked tongue.

"Hello," she replied as bravely as she could.

"May I speak with your parents?"

"No," she said. Her instincts were telling her to shut the door in the man's face and phone someone who could help.

"Well, I've come to collect some stolen property. Your parents know I am coming for it; I spoke with your mother this morning. You mind if I come in and find it? Then I'll be on my way."

Jillian blocked his entry to the house. "I'm not letting you in." She took her medallion from her pocket and hung it around her neck, where Nicholas could see it.

"I see," Nicholas sneered unhappily. "It looks like you are under the protection of one of the Secret People, now. Very well, I'll play along. One of them is watching us, anyway."

Jillian saw Olivet Omari's silhouette, standing on the roof of a neighbour's house. She stood a little straighter.

"What do you want," Nicholas said.

"I want a chance to authenticate my discovery before I hand the telescope back to you."

Nicholas laughed. "Such big and grown-up words."

Jillian stepped forward and said, "You represent The Guardians, right? I read about them on the internet today. They do education development work, right? That's what you were doing at my school yesterday: offering money for new computers."

"That's right," Nicholas confirmed.

"So, if you say the telescope belongs to the Guardians, and the Guardians are big supporters of education, why don't you *lend* the telescope to me for a while? I need it for a school project. I'll give it back when I'm finished."

Nicholas pursed his lips and sighed. "How long will that take?"

"One more night," she told him.

"Then I'm going to stay here until you're done," Nicholas insisted.

"Meet me in the back yard," Jillian told him, and then she shut the door in his face. When she heard his footsteps wander off, she leaned her back on the door and remembered to breathe. She smiled; she had won her first victory.

To reward herself, or perhaps prepare for the next confrontation with Nicholas, she took one of her mother's suit jackets, and a pair of her mother's nylons. She put it on, and gave herself a brief moment to admire her new image in the mirror, and to make Nicholas wait.

When she brought the chest with the telescope into the back yard, Nicholas was impatiently pacing on the grass and knocking his walking-stick on deck rails and flower pots, waiting for her. Jillian set the telescope on its tripod and fixed its axis-wheels to their start positions. The telescope looked more complicated now. Black metal coils and bands clamped around the telescope's main cylinder. More dials, knobs, and switches stuck out from the axis wheels.

Nicholas shone his flashlight on the telescope, saying, "Well, there's the contraption itself, at last."

Jillian stood in his way. "Please, we need darkness for the telescope to work properly," she warned him. Nicholas dutifully put his light away, although he grumbled about it.

"How long will this take," he complained.

"Just a minute," Jillian answered. She attached a lens on the eyepiece which would project images from the telescope on to a screen, for everyone to see.

"You can help, actually," Jillian suggested. "You can write a letter to my teacher, and to the Secret University, saying you saw all the same things that I saw."

"The only reason I'm here is to collect my client's stolen property when you're done with it," Nicholas told her.

Jillian bowed her head slightly, to look up at him with her biggest, brownest upturned eyes, and said, "But don't you care about education, Mr. Brogger? Your clients do, don't they?"

Nicholas sighed and folded his arms, and looked away. He saw that Olivet was now watching from the roof of Jillian's own house, and that at least one more silhouette had joined her. He said, "Of course we care about education. How can I help."

"Thank you, sir!" Jillian squealed, and she rewarded him with her brightest and happiest smile, and a twirl of her hair with her finger. "So, you can start by taking this bed sheet, and hanging it on the clothesline. We're going to use it as a screen."

Nicholas hung the bed sheet on the clothesline.

"Next, I need you to write a short description of everything that comes up. Take pictures, too."

Nicholas took a lawn chair from the deck and sat it down at a place where he would get a good view of the screen. He took a notepad from his briefcase, and grumbled, "All right, then. Let's get this done."

Jillian smiled again. She said, "Let's start by calibrating the telescope. To show that I'm using it properly. Take this-" she handed Nicholas the atlas, "- and pick three things in it for me to find. When that's done we can look at the moon, to see if we can confirm my discovery."

Nicholas muttered to himself as he flipped the pages of the atlas. Then he said, "This is a first edition. It's very valuable. How did you get it?"

"Library book," she said.

Nicholas frowned, but said nothing more about it. He scanned the pages of the atlas some more, to pick something especially difficult for Jillian to find. When he was ready, he said, "All right, find the Azimov Cluster."

"Easy-peasy," Jillian crowed, and she set to work. She turned her back to Nicholas because she didn't want him to see the worry that fell on her face. Even with the help of the atlas, finding something she herself had never found before would not be easy. Yet what she worried about most was his professed ability to detect lies.

She glanced around to Nicholas, to see what he was doing. He was talking to someone on his cellphone.

"No, I haven't got it yet," he said to whomever he was calling. "It seems that the previous owners are contesting our jurisdiction. I was forced to parlay with a little girl. It's absurd, I know! But some of the Secret People are watching me now. What can I do?"

Jillian pretended to ignore him.

From studying the atlas, she got a general idea of where to find the Azimov Cluster. She set the axis wheels to the co-ordinates, and checked the range finder. It showed three different clusters with gaseous nebula spread through them. One of them had to be the right one. Remembering that the cluster was named after a writer, she set the third axis wheel on the book symbol, and then checked the range finder again. This time, just as she hoped, she found a cluster which vaguely resembled the face of a man with thick-rimmed glasses and grey sideburns.

"Yes!" she cheered. And she flipped the switch to project the image on to the screen. "See, mister Brogger! There it is!"

"There it is," he acknowledged. He snatched the atlas away again, and said, "But that one was too easy."

As she waited for him to choose her next target, she noticed shadows gathering on the rooftops of nearby houses, and on the tops of the tallest trees. More of the Secret People, she assumed. Yet their attention, however supportive, would not make her work any easier.

"Now try to find The Cubic Zirconia Planet of Beta Reticulum," Nicholas told her.

"But that constellation is in the southern hemisphere! And we're in Canada! I can't look straight through the earth!"

"You want me as your witness that you're using the thing properly? All settings aligned right, all lenses angled and focused? Find something only a professional could find."

Jillian pouted for a moment, and then got to work. She swiveled the various knobs and winches and axis-wheels around, unsure at first of what to do. She turned the telescope toward her own face and looked at her reflection in the lens. For a moment she imagined she was holding her telescope for the last time. Then she remembered reading in the atlas about fields of space ice which glittered in the light of nearby stars. She wondered if it was possible to find the planet by looking for its reflection in one of those fields, just as she was looking at her own reflection in the lens. With some help from the atlas, she pointed the telescope to a field of space ice that might be in the right position to reflect the image of her target.

Nicholas snickered again. "Clever girl, but not clever enough."

"I'm not finished yet!" she rebuffed him. Then she picked up her cellphone, to access the internet.

"You won't find the target on the internet," Nicholas warned her.

"I know. I'm just looking up the atomic mass of cubic zirconia."

And then she stuck out her tongue at him. Nicholas responded by folding his arms and turning away.

When she found the information she needed, she gently nudged the third axis ring until its indicator pointed at the number 123.218, the molar mass of zirconium dioxide. In a flash, the shining image of the Cubic Zirconia Planet was projected on the screen, though the image was fragmented by the ice field that reflected it.

Nicholas pursed his lips and said, "Too clever for your own good."

Jillian glanced quickly at Professor Omari, who was still watching from the roof of the house. She smiled, and nodded approvingly. The hooded and cloaked silhouettes of other observers, some floating on Persian carpets, some seated on levitating boats, one seated in a cooking pot that floated in a bubble, also seemed to approve. Some of them applauded.

Nicholas stood up from his chair, studied the audience for a moment, then said, "Well, I think we can all agree that the telescope is working properly. So let's cut to the chase. Show me the money-shot. The people you say you found on the moon. But I know you won't find them. Because they don't exist. And therefore—" and Nicholas left the end of his sentence unspoken. He smirked at Jillian, and lit a cigarette.

Pointing the telescope at the moon was easy. The problem was in seeing it differently. Time had passed, and more of the moon was covered in sunlight now. She angled the telescope to the slice of the lunar disk still in shadow, and then she tested the lenses and knobs and wheels to see if she could make the lights of the lunar cities reappear. Most of the time, however, her efforts caused the telescope to wander off target, and focus on something to one side or another.

Brendan Myers

Nicholas, meanwhile, was already declaring victory. Addressing the shadowy audience around him, he declared: "She doesn't know what she's doing! You may as well admit that the world of the moon-people is a fraud, and let me take the telescope and be on my way."

Olivet Omari floated down from her perch on the roof of the house and said, "Mister Brogger, this artifact isn't really yours, is it?"

Nicholas nodded. "In point of fact, it belongs to my clients. The Guardians International Organization."

"And I hear you told Jillian's parents that it was stolen."

"I did. And it was."

"Stolen from my University. By *you*. And then given to the Guardians, who claimed some kind of legal domain over it."

A flurry of whispers rose and fell from the onlookers.

Nicholas had a counter accusation for Olivet ready. "So after that, you stole it from the Guardians, didn't you? And then you gave it to this child, where you thought we wouldn't look for it."

Olivet didn't deny Nicholas' accusation. She said, "Why did you steal it in the first place? What do you plan to do with it?"

"It doesn't matter what we plan to do with it," Nicholas shouted. "It's ours, and it's none of your business if we lock it in a bank vault or crush it under a rock."

Nicholas' comment drew a flurry of shocked whispers from the audience.

Olivet gasped out her objection: "You would destroy an Ethereal Cosmographic Telescope? There's only seven of them in the world! Have you no sense of its value?"

"I know it's value. That feather-brained philosopher who invented it thought he could use it to see all the forces of nature, all the strings of time and space— even to read the mind of God! But he never found that better world he was looking for. Because it isn't there! And that's why the Guardians have to— wait just one bloody minute! I know what you're doing! You're trying to give Jillian more time."

Jillian was trying to ignore their conversation as she worked, but she heard Nicholas say she was out of her time. It reminded her of something that Johnny-o had found when he was perusing the Atlas, about how the rotation of the earth was part of the telescope's mechanism.

"That's what I was doing wrong when I couldn't find it! Now all I need to do is figure out how to set the position of the time-wheel to account for the rotation of the earth– and then see the moon as it might be in the future, not just as it might be today–"

At the top of the tripod, but just hidden beneath the joints and balance-weights that held the telescope in place, there was one last hidden knob, shaped like a sundial. She turned it slowly as she watched the moon's face in the rangefinder. What she saw made her wonder if the telescope was also a kind of time machine. One by one, little sparks and candles of light appeared in the lunar shadows. Soon they were joined by more precious lights, forming small clusters at first, then growing into larger clusters. And then a few fragile dotted lines spread across the surface, joining the clusters together. Jillian grinned, full of pride, as she flipped the lever that projected the image on to the screen, for everyone to see.

The shadowy audience cheered and clapped and shouted Jillian's name. Many of them descended from their perches to shake her hand. Olivet hugged her.

Nicholas stood with arms folded, and face frowning. He stared silently at the image of the moon on the screen, glittering with cities and railways and launch pads. Then he glared at Jillian.

"You've had your fun. You found your Moon People. I'll sign off on the discovery, just like I promised. Now package the thing up and give it back to me."

"Fine, it's yours," Jillian whined, and she stepped behind the screen. She flipped a few of the switches and knobs on the telescope. The screen went dark again.

Olivet presented Nicholas with a contract on official Secret University of Anatolia letterhead.

"Sign here to confirm that you are a witness to the discovery," she told him. Nicholas signed the contract and pushed it on her chest. Olivet took it, and shook her head at him.

Jillian took down the bedsheet and revealed the telescope, disassembled and neatly stowed in its antique wooden chest. Nicholas stepped up to it, and shined his camera-light into it again. He glanced at the black metal bands clamped on the bronze cylinder, and dials and buttons, and the tripod legs, all in their place. Jillian shut the lid of the chest, snapped the lock in place, and handed it to him.

Nicholas studied her face for a moment, and furrowed his brow. "There's something you're not telling me," he said.

"I was just— just hoping you would let me keep it longer," Jillian said. "After all, it wasn't *me* who stole it. What are you going to do with it?"

"What do you think?" he replied. He marched off with it, followed by Jillian, Olivet, and some of the Secret People. He put it down in the middle of the road, near his car, and opened it. From the trunk of his car he produced an orange plastic jerrycan containing a sick-smelling liquid, which he poured into the chest.

"What the hell are you doing!" Olivet demanded.

"This is for your own good," Nicholas said. Then he lit a match and tossed it into the chest.

A fireball burst forth, and almost engulfed Nicholas himself, as well as the lower branches of nearby trees. Outrage and anger howled from every witness. Jillian shrieked, and hid her face.

Olivet ran to the burning chest, and then ran to Nicholas, shouting incoherently: "Nicholas! You–you–why the hell did you do that!"

"Like I said. It's for your own good," he answered. Then he casually photographed his handiwork, saluted Jillian, and strolled back to his car.

Olivet swung her fist at him, although he dodged it easily, as her attack was too angry to be focused. But Nicholas soon saw that she was not the only one drawing near with angry intent. He dashed into his car as fast as his hobbled gait could carry him, and drove away.

Olivet shouted to Jillian, "Get a bucket of water!"

Jillian had been watching from the front porch of her house. She had gripped the railing so tightly that her knuckles were white. Only when Nicholas' car turned around a corner did she let go of it, and breathe normally again. She closed her eyes, and then she smiled.

"Jillian? Water!" Olivet commanded again.

Jillian turned around and picked up a cardboard box that she had hidden just around the corner of her house. She put it down on the grass, and opened it. The light of the fire glinted from an antique bronze cylinder within.

Olivet smiled, and then laughed. "Jillian! How did you— oh! I thought the telescope looked a little different just now."

Jillian said, "I discovered yesterday that Nicholas didn't know what the telescope really looked like. So, I made another one."

All around her, the shadows of the Secret People cheered again. Jillian beamed with pride, and ran forward to hug her professor. Then she picked up the telescope and held it high for all the Secret People to see. They applauded for her again, and Jillian laughed, and twirled around, and laughed again.

*   *   *

A short while later, after Olivet put out the burning chest with the garden hose, and the Secret People had dispersed, Jillian sat on the roof of the abandoned house. She looked over the village, with its tall maples and ashes and elms, some shadowed and some brightened by the golden glow from streetlights, or from the windows of houses where someone remained awake.

"The old chest was an antique, as well," Olivet observed.

"I'm sorry," said Jillian.

"Don't be. You saved the important part."

"The original tripod was in there, too," Jillian explained. "I didn't know how to build another one. And I didn't have much time."

Olivet sighed, and decided the loss was an acceptable sacrifice. She said, "Nicholas will eventually figure out that he destroyed a fake."

"Yeah, I know," Jillian agreed. "I suppose you will have to hide the real one somewhere else, now."

Olivet nodded, and said, "I'll let you hang on to it for a few more days. After that, I might have something else you can keep safe for me, for a little while."

Jillian smiled softly, and then tilted her head back, to consider the stars, and to imagine what else might some day be discovered out there.

*   *   *

A week later, after dinner, another heavy knock on the door announced another package for Jillian.

"This is getting a little silly," said her mother.

The new package looked like a bolt of cloth, about as long as Jillian was tall, and tied with coarse ropes. Jillian ran with it into the back yard before her parents could see what it was. She unwrapped it, and discovered Professor Olivet's flying carpet.

She cheered out loud, and looked up to the sky and said, "Thank you professor!"

She spread it on the grass, and sat on it, and grasped it by two of its corners. Slowly, it raised itself just above the ground. Jillian soon found that by shifting her weight and leaning one way or another, she could steer it, and speed up, and slow down. It would take a bit of practice, she knew; but she was excited now, and was already choosing the places she wanted to visit.

Her parents entered the back yard just in time to see her flying off in the direction of the conservation park outside of town, and to hear the sound of her delighted voice, yowling and laughing all the way.

~ the end ~

~ A Note About The Story ~

A Trick Of The Light is a spinoff story from the world of
Fellwater and The Hidden Houses, my urban fantasy series. I
wanted to explore areas of the world not seen in the main series.
I also wanted to write something that might bring together my
two favourite interests from when I was the same age as my
heroine: fairy tales, and astronomy. And after living in west
Quebec for several years, I found myself feeling nostalgic for
my home town, Elora Ontario, the village which serves as the
model for my fictional town of Fellwater.

When I was a child, an empty and partially run-down house
stood in my neighbourhood, just along the line where the
century-houses ended and the postwar bungalows began. My
sisters and I sometimes made up stories about ghosts who lived
in it. The house was eventually refurbished and inhabited, so the
house became no longer scary, so we stopped telling those
stories. Some thirty years later, I found a similar old house near
my apartment here in Gatineau, similarly surrounded by trees
and by postwar bungalows. Then the story of that house in Elora
returned to me.

For my seventh or maybe eighth birthday, I can't quite recall,
my dad gave me a copy of *Our Universe* by Roy Gallant, and I
read it so voraciously that the pages started falling out. I still
have that book, more than thirty years later, although some of its
pages are now missing. Back then I also had a telescope of my
own, although I mostly used it to look at sunspots: an attachment
projected the image of the sun on to a white metal plate. I liked
to imagine that I was a scientist or an explorer, studying the sun
from a spacecraft in high orbit. The idea of a story about a magic
telescope, accompanied by a magic atlas, secretly delivered to a
curious but not necessarily well-behaved child, had been on my
mind for many years.

I had other influences, of course. Readers of the first edition
noted a similarity with Phillip Pullman's *His Dark Materials*
series. I had read *The Golden Compass* before writing Jillian
Brighton, and it made me want to write a childhood wonder-tale
with a hint of adult concern. (But I didn't want to write 'fanfic';
I wanted to stay in my own world.) By the way, Jillian's theft of
her mother's nylons is a tip of the hat, of a sort, to a remark
about Susan Pevensie in C.S. Lewis' *The Last Battle*. But I leave
it to the investigative reader to discover what that was all about.

The real impetus to put pen to paper came in December of 2013, when my partner asked me to write her a story for Christmas, instead of buying her a regular gift. I wrote the first draft in two weeks. With her permission, I later self-published it under the title *Jillian Brighton and the Wonderful Cosmographic Telescope.* This edition in your hands is what happened to it after I ran a crowd-funding campaign to pay for a professional editor for my Hidden Houses series. The editor liked the main character and the story's premise very much, but he felt that acts two and three needed a complete overhaul. So, during October and November of 2014, I overhauled them. Jillian's teacher and parents became less prominent. A dark and perhaps dystopian ending was removed. (Perhaps I should say, 'saved for later.') Still, after the editor signed off on the text, the length of the story was about 1,600 words *longer* than the first edition. This is very unusual in an editing process. But I think the result is a much better story.

There are more tales to tell in the world of The Hidden Houses, and there are more Secret People to meet. The work of writing the fourth and final volume of the main series is in progress. Other spinoff stories are planned, as well. Now that Jillian has the professor's magic carpet, who knows where it will take her!

Please visit my web site to explore other titles in the series, and to be the first to know about future releases.

Web: BrendanMyers.net, and Fellwater.ca

Twitter: @Fellwater

And **thank you** for supporting my work!

~ Other Titles in The Hidden Houses series ~

Part One: Fellwater

"Fellwater" is a modern fantasy novel about two lovers caught between two rival factions of an ancient secret society.

On the night Katie tried to tell Eric her true feelings, all they did was argue, and she left with a broken heart. But then she met Carlo, a charming, cosmopolitan, and mysterious man from an Italian noble house. In his presence a mystical vision overtook her, and she remembered meeting him before, thousands of years ago, in the ancient Celtic iron age. But she awoke the following morning in a hospital, without knowing how she got there, and she learned that Eric spent the night in jail after being chased by gunmen. All was not as it seemed, and they were both in terrible danger.

"*Myers' characters inhabit a world rich with political intrigue; the machinations of aristocratic families descended from ancient gods. Fellwater is taut, poignant, and imaginative.*"
- Jordan Stratford,
author of *Mechanicals* and *Wollstonecraft*.

"*Brendan Myers has taken his deep understanding of the Celtic culture and created a world as riveting as George R.R. Martin's Game of Thrones.*"
- Yvonne Erlichman, God Box Cafe.

Part Two: Hallowstone

As Eric mourns his lover's death, a flamboyant stranger draws him into a conspiracy to destroy a magical well.

The death of Eric's lover left him grief-stricken for months. So when the smooth-talking Heathcliff claimed to have spoken with Katie's ghost, Eric wanted to hear more. He followed Heathcliff to Hallowstone Castle, where a seer told him that Katie had been murdered. Meanwhile, a magical well in Fellwater Grove comes under attack. Eric volunteers to help investigate the attackers, but the more he learns about the true nature of the well, the more his loyalties are put to the test, and the deeper he falls into danger. Without knowing who to trust, and without time to heal his grief, Eric must find Katie's killer, and face a momentous choice.

"The characters in this series are distinct, rich with depth, and you are left with a sense that they all have a long history that have led them up to this point in the story... The story keeps you on the edge of your seat, waiting to find out who will reveal their true nature right until the end."

- John David Hickey, storyteller,
author of *Shortening the Road.*

Part Three: Clan Fianna

Accused of a crime he didn't commit, Eric is banished from his clan. But in exile he discovers a secret that threatens everyone he loves.

Eric is the first 'outsider' in 300 years to be made an honorary member of Clan Brigantia. But when an ambassador from a rival house accuses Eric of poisoning his wife, Eric is banished from the clan. Meanwhile, packs of monsters are escaping from their prisons in the underworld, and threatening the village of Fellwater. And a powerful but mysterious social movement called the Guardians claims that they have been secretly protecting the world from such creatures for centuries. Eric discovers a dangerous truth about the monsters: but his former friends, convinced of his guilt, don't believe him. Burdened by loneliness, and the false charges on his head, Eric struggles to clear his name and warn his friends of the threat to their home.

"It is an ensemble cast piece, with a great sense of each of the major characters being at the centre of their own story, with all of these individual threads weaving a great and complex tapestry of plot. This immediately brings to mind comparisons with Robert Jordan and George R. R. Martin, but for my taste this book exceeds much of the work of both of these super-luminaries..."

- J. J. Colvin, review on Amazon.co.uk

~ About the Author ~

Brendan Myers is a professor of philosophy at Cégep Heritage College, in Gatineau, Quebec. He's a TED speaker, a game designer, an occasional musician, and the author of fifteen books, in fiction and nonfiction. He loves space exploration and fairy tales. He lives in a library, next door to a forest.

Find him on the web at BrendanMyers.net

Follow him on Twitter @Fellwater

~ Other titles by Brendan Myers ~

The Hidden Houses series:

Fellwater
Hallowstone
Clan Fianna
The Seekers

Non-fiction:

The Other Side of Virtue
Loneliness and Revelation
Circles of Meaning, Labyrinths of Fear
The Earth, The Gods, and The Soul

All titles are available from major online retailers, and can be ordered through your local bookstore.

www.ingramcontent.com/pod-product-compliance
Lightning Source LLC
Chambersburg PA
CBHW020650130626
46552CB00003B/1485